It Wasn't Me

Classic series from Michael Bond:

Paddington Bear
Olga da Polga
Monsieur Pamplemousse

MICHAEL BOND

It Wasn't Me

illustrated by Joel Stewart

DOUBLEDAY

DOUBLEDAY

UK | USA | Canada | Ireland | Australia
India | New Zealand | South Africa

Doubleday is part of the Penguin Random House group of companies
whose addresses can be found at global.penguinrandomhouse.com.

www.penguin.co.uk
www.puffin.co.uk
www.ladybird.co.uk

This edition published 2016

001

Set in Century Schoolbook
Printed in Great Britain by Clays Ltd, St Ives plc

A CIP catalogue record for this book is available from the British Library

Hardback ISBN: 978–0–857–53430–9
Trade paperback ISBN: 978–0–552–57313–9

All correspondence to:
Doubleday
Penguin Random House Children's
80 Strand, London WC2R 0RL

To the original Harry,
dearly loved despite everything

A note from the author

Most leading characters in works of fiction
are modelled on real people, and in committing
that fact to paper the author usually goes to
endless trouble to make sure their personal details
remain hidden from view so that no one will
recognize them. While I was writing this book
I was able to enjoy the luxury of making sure
the reverse was true. In short, what you read
says it all. There is nothing added and nothing
taken away. It is simply Harry all the way.

Michael Bond

1

Never Fear – Harry's Here

'Fancy Harry saying you can recognize his grandfather from a mile away because he has lots of white hair with a hole in the middle!'

Hearing Dad's voice coming from the next room, I pricked up my ears – Harry being the key word, of course, because it happens to be my name.

'It was only an essay,' said Mum.

'Only an essay!' Dad gave a loud snort. 'Well, it's your father. But you know who to blame if everyone starts pointing him out next time he goes to a school concert; like they did with me when he concocted that story about my being in the fire brigade.

'"How very interesting, Mr Manners . . ."' Dad went into his 'Miss Spooner the Headmistress' routine. '"You must come and give a talk to the fifth form one  of these days. We would all love to hear what it's like. Do you spend much of your time up a ladder?"'

'I really don't know what made him do it,' admitted Mum. 'I suppose he must have been reading something about them at the time. Anyway, it's not his fault he happens to be blessed with a vivid imagination.'

I'll say this for Mum. She always sticks up for me.

'Remember that parents' evening when the geography teacher told us that Harry had been keeping the whole class enthralled with the story of how we'd been rescued by a helicopter during a snowstorm on the Cairngorms?' said Dad. 'We've never been within a hundred miles of the Cairngorms. The trouble is, we have to suffer. I shall never hear the last of it if they get to know about it in the office.'

'I think it's all wrong,' said Mum, 'getting children to write an essay about their home life. I suppose the teachers do it so that they can get to know them better.'

'Find out about things that are none of

their business, more like.' Dad sounded a bit disgruntled. He's a funny person, my dad. I don't mean funny laugh-out-loud – I mean funny peculiar. Once he gets his teeth into something, he goes on and on about it. Meal times are the worst. There's no escape then. He says things like: 'If we'd been meant to eat peas with a knife, they'd have made them with dents on the blade.'

I think eating's boring – especially when it's peas. It makes it more interesting if you try to see how many you can balance on a knife at one go. I once got up to thirty-two before Dad noticed, and that was only because he shouted and it made me jump so much, they all rolled off onto the floor! Even then I only found twenty-seven. The rest got trampled into the carpet.

Breakfast time is the worst; especially when I'm in a hurry to get to school. Or, to put it another way, when I'm late for school and Mum keeps telling me to get a move on.

Dad comes out with things like: 'Must you use your hand as a shovel? Why can't you use a spoon like any normal child?'

I bet he was just as bad when he was small. 'I was thinking only the other day at breakfast, "cornflakes" is a funny name for a food – it sounds like something that's come away from your foot.'

'Must you?' said my Big Sister, pretending to throw up.

That did it. I'd had enough. My Big Sister's right about one thing. She says listeners never hear any good about themselves, and at times like that it's best to be alone in your room.

That's one of the good things about having an untidy bedroom. People don't come in and start poking around. With mine they usually open the door, say something like 'Ugh!' then go away again.

Having made myself comfortable, I went back to my Max Masters.

There's nothing like a good book. They make pictures in your head. At least, they do in mine. I remember reading one written by someone called Ray Bradbury. It was about a machine that could take you on a trip back in time. The only trouble was, you weren't allowed to touch anything. In the story someone accidentally killed a butterfly, and when the passengers returned home, they found the whole world had changed. I could picture it all.

Max Masters's book features a boy about the same age as me, whose mother sends him out to buy some chips.

He comes across a shop called Chips with Everything. What he doesn't realize is that they aren't the sort of chips you eat with fish; they are computer chips.

There are some 486s and a whole host of 283s, which are now so old I don't even have one in my tablet. But best of all, there are a lot of Pentium chips. Imagine, all that for tenpence! The man in the shop says they fell off the back of a lorry that very morning.

It made me laugh because in the story the boy couldn't help trying one to see what it tasted like and it stuck in his throat. After which he began saying all kinds of weird things like: 'Did you know that if the average man was freeze dried and then vacuum packed, he would only be a third of his normal weight?'

He wouldn't be much use to anyone, of course, but I think it's interesting all the same.

What I like most about Max Masters's books is that they're full of facts and figures. The sort of things that stick in your mind; not like the ones they try and teach you at school. I bet people remember King Alfred because he burned the cakes long after they've forgotten what date it was.

However, it started me thinking. I mean, suppose someone who didn't know anything about computers ate a whole packet of Pentium chips by mistake. And then, supposing, just supposing, they all joined up inside and made one ginormous computer. Think of all the problems he would be able to solve. Imagine being able to walk in the front door one day and say something like: 'What's two thousand, seven hundred and thirty-four multiplied by two million, five hundred and thirty-two?' and come up with the right answer.

I know what my dad would say. 'Go and wash your mouth out,' or 'Do be quiet. It's Arsenal playing.'

My Big Sister's lips would go all pursed. Especially if Dad came running in with a pencil and paper, having woken up to the fact that I'd got the answer right after all.

That would set Mum off. First of all she would take my temperature and then she would send for the doctor – just in case I was sickening for something.

Lying back on my bed, I closed my eyes so that I could picture it better. I bet they would soon be sorry they'd grumbled at me. I imagined the doctor telling me to say 'Aaah' like he always does. Dad says it's so that he can check up in his Home Doctor while you're not looking, but my Big Sister reckons it's to stop me talking. She would!

Anyway, that's when I showed him. Instead of saying 'Aaah', I came out with Einstein's formula for relativity.

'Would you mind repeating that?' said the doctor.

'Of course,' I replied. 'I'll go through it backwards if you like.' I wouldn't mind betting the same sort of thing happened to Einstein himself. That's how things get discovered. I think a lot of things get discovered by accident.

Mrs Einstein probably called out, 'Dinner's ready, Albert . . . Don't let yours get cold.' And he came out with his formula

without thinking. Mum often says that if I'd been born a few years earlier, I would most likely have discovered penicillin. I'm not sure what she means by that.

'I think I may have got pneumonoultramicroscopicsilicovolcanoconiosis,' I said to the doctor.

Well, you could have heard a pin drop. (I first came across the word when I was looking up how to spell pneumatic. It had taken me half the morning. I'd been looking through the 'n's. Well, how was I to know it started with a 'p'? I think they should have special dictionaries showing words the way they look as though should be spelled. Otherwise how are you supposed to look them up?)

The doctor gave me a hard look, then turned to Dad. 'I'll write out a prescription for some tablets,' he said. 'Tell him to take them three times a day before meals. If it doesn't go away in three days, call me again.'

From that moment on a sort of chain reaction set in. I think he must have told some of his other patients about it while he was doing his rounds, because the news spread like wildfire.

The very next day there was a phone call from a newspaper. And before you could say 'om-bom-stiggy-woggles' or, as my sister would say, 'awesome', there I was, all over the front page of the *Sun*.

Mum had palpitations and Dad couldn't believe his eyes. 'I've fathered a genius!' he said, taking the credit.

'And who mothered it?' asked Mum. 'Who brought it up? Washed it? Fed it? Read to it? Listened to it whining for hours on end, day in, day out?

'Goodnight,' she said as she tucked me in. 'Sleep tight.'

'In Shakespeare's time,' I said, 'mattresses were secured to the bed-frames by a rope. When the rope was pulled, it tightened everything up. That's where the saying comes from.'

'There he goes again!' groaned Dad.

I closed my eyes as tight as possible and took a deep breath, holding it as long as I could.

I won't bore you with all that happened after that: the television and radio appearances; the quiz shows (Jeremy Paxman wanted my autograph!); an interview with the Prime Minister – he came to see me, and the chauffeur parked his car right outside the house (or rather, he tried to, but Dad's old Rover was in the way); articles in all the newspapers – and not just English ones – WORLDWIDE! An American magazine called *Time* even had my picture on its front cover.

And then it happened.

I got kidnapped by three men from a FOREIGN POWER. I knew they were from a foreign power because they had beards and spoke in a funny way.

It was when I came across this strange-looking car parked in our road. I stopped to have a closer look because I'd never seen one quite like it before. One of the men asked me if I would like to see in the boot. The next thing I knew I was locked inside it.

We drove for 2.32 miles. I knew it was 2.32 miles because I counted the number of bumps. We live on one of those concrete roads in the suburbs of London with bumps between the sections. If you know the distance between them, it's easy peasy to work out.

The men were a bit upset when I told them. 'I suppose you know vhere ve hov taken you?' said the leader.

'Just behind the brewery,' I said. 'You can smell the malt fumes from a mile away.'

'You vant to vatch people don't smell you a mile away,' he said. 'It can be arranged. It's like I say. You vant to mind your Ps and Qs.'

'It's interesting you should say that when we're near a brewery,' I said, 'because that's how the saying came about. In the old days, people drank their beer out of pint glasses and quart tankards, and when they got noisy the landlord used to shout out: "Watch your Ps and Qs!"'

After that they put some sticking

plaster over my mouth and went into the next room, so I kept myself occupied by pretending I was still at home and carried on making myself useful, as usual.

I retuned the television set for them, but somehow it ended up with all the buttons getting the same channel, so I tried out the sound system. Then that got stuck at FULL BLAST. It wasn't my fault. I wasn't anywhere near it. The trouble was, the volume-control knob fell off and rolled out of sight. I couldn't find it anywhere.

'Why did you do that?' I asked as the men came rushing into the room and the chief one pulled off my sticking plaster. It was the first time I noticed he had a twitch in one eye.

'Vy! Vy! Vy!' he said. 'Vy do you keep asking vy?'

'Vy do you vant to know?' I asked.

He couldn't answer that.

Instead, he put the sticking plaster back on and left it there until next morning at breakfast. I had a lot bottled up by then and it all came pouring out, until one of them pushed something called a cross ant into my mouth. To my surprise it was made of flaky pastry and was surprisingly tasty. But then again, when you're hungry you'll eat anything.

Now, I don't know about you, but I like strawberry jam, and there was this big jar of it on the other side of the table. All three of the men let out a shout as I made a grab for it. But they weren't quick enough. I beat them to it by a mile.

'That tablecloth was fresh on this morning,' grumbled the leader.

'It wasn't my fault,' I said. 'How was I

supposed to know the lid wasn't screwed on?'

'The jam fell out all by itself, I suppose,' said one of the others. He reminded me a bit of my dad.

'Sorry,' I said as I tried to put it back in the jar.

'Do you have to do it with your fingers?' asked the big one. 'Can't you use a spoon?'

'God gave us fingers to use,' I said.

'That's all we need,' he said. 'A religious maniac!'

Now, you may not believe this, but with that he buried his face in his hands and began to cry. A grown man! I felt really sorry for him and patted him on the back, but that only seemed to make matters worse.

'My best suit!' he shouted. 'Now you've got jam all over it!' Well, it wasn't so much a shout; it was a sort of wail, like the noise a dog makes when you tread on its tail by mistake.

Soon after that they let me go. I wasn't sorry, I can tell you. It was worse than being at home. Still, I shook hands with the leader before I left.

All he said was: 'Ugh!' Just like people do when they come into my bedroom . . .

As I opened my eyes, I realized that

it was my Big Sister. I thought he had
sounded a bit girlish.

'You've been having
one of your dreams
again,' she said. 'And
what's that empty jam
jar doing in your bed? It's
gone everywhere!'

'What have you been
up to?' said Mum when I
went downstairs. 'We were
beginning to get worried.'

'I've been thinking,' I
said.

'Oh dear,' said Dad. 'I don't like the
sound of that.'

As luck would have it, just at that
moment a big black Mercedes with tinted
windows drew up outside.

'I wonder who that can be,' said Mum.

'It might be the Prime Minister,' I said carelessly. 'He probably wants to seek my advice about something or other.' I tapped the side of my nose like they do in films. 'It may be TOP SECRET. I'd better see him in the front room.'

'If it is the Prime Minister,' said my Big Sister sarcastically as she peered through a gap in the curtains, 'he must be hungry after his long drive from Downing Street. He's eating his sandwiches.'

That's typical of her. She's got no imagination. 'He's probably come from his country home in the Chilterns,' I said. 'It's no wonder he needs a bite to eat.'

'At least we shall have a bit of peace and quiet,' said Dad, picking up his paper. 'When I was your age, boys were meant to be seen and not heard.'

Can you believe it? I bet if I was struck

dumb one day he'd be sorry. Mind you, I tried it once, just to see what happened. I said to him: 'I've been pretending to be struck dumb for three whole days and you didn't even notice.'

All he said was: 'I thought it was too good to be true.'

Well, see if I care. I don't mind if nobody believes me. I've got pictures in my head to prove it. One day someone will invent a machine so that I can plug myself in and print them all out. Then they'll be sorry.

In the meantime, have I ever told you how I was given the nickname Fingers Galore? If you'd like to know, read on.

2

The Spirit of Christmas

My Big Sister has had it in for me ever since the day when she was small and Mum asked her if she would like a new brother or sister to play with, or whether she would prefer it if they bought a second television.

She was into dolls at the time, so she said 'Yes' straight away to the first choice. Now she wishes she'd voted for a new television, especially when I'm watching something like *Top Gear* and there's a fashion programme on the other channel.

She's the one who came up with her own nickname for me – 'Fingers Galore'. It was just before Christmas last year. 'Fingers for short,' she said, 'but hopefully not for long.'

Meaning, I suppose, that if I'm not careful I shan't see my tenth birthday next year. Just because I'd opened all the doors on her advent calendar to see what was underneath. I bet if I wasn't around any more she'd be sorry. I bet she'd cry herself to sleep. Big sisters are like that. I might try disappearing one day, just to see what happens. I bet her pillow would be sopping wet by morning and the feathers would go hard and she'd wake up with ear-ache, which would serve her right.

The trouble with nicknames is, once people start using them they're hard to get rid of. Though first names you've been landed with are even worse. I think children should be allowed a trial period, and when they get to the age of eight they can start afresh if they want to.

Reg Dwight is a good example. I don't know how old he was when he changed his name to Elton John, but look where it got him!

Apparently when my dad first started going out with Mum, she had a thing about the royal family. Before I was born she had a big crush on Prince Harry, but she wasn't alone in that: he'd been voted the sexiest man in the world. Apparently Dad used to say he was all right if you like that kind of thing, but when she wanted to call me Harry, he couldn't stand it any longer.

However, he took a close look at me

and said, 'A miss is as good as a mile,' and he looked much happier after that.

Prince Harry was on the early evening news the other day and in my rush to see what all the fuss was about, the brightness knob came away in my hand. Just like the one belonging to the kidnappers in my dream. That's the trouble with knobs – they're always coming off. I think they must all be made by the same people. I was about to hide ours under an armchair when, as ill luck would have it, Dad arrived home.

'Oh!' he shouted as he picked it up. 'What have we here? A flying knob. We seem to be plagued by them in this house. And I bet I know who was nowhere near this one when it fell off.'

Mind you, that dates our television as well. There aren't many sets with knobs on these days. Dad thinks that's why they invented the remote control – because it's easier than making knobs that don't come away in your hand.

He says there's nothing 'remote' about ours. It's much too handy for his liking. In his view it has to be the worst invention ever. 'Some people, mentioning no names' – but he was looking at me when he said it – 'some Button Pressers will keep changing channels every five seconds.'

I suppose I'm lucky in a way. Most people only have one name for the whole of their life, but I've got lots.

If you ask me, that's why babies cry in church when they're being baptized. They simply don't like the sound of their name and don't fancy hearing it repeated for the rest of their life.

Anyway, back to my being called

Harry. I happen to like it myself. I'm not sure what I would change my name to if I became really famous.

The reason I'm telling you all this is because I was given a John Wayne cowboy outfit last Christmas, which is how I came by the nickname Trigger for a while.

Now you may well ask who or what was John Wayne and I must admit he was before my time, so it wasn't  until I read about him on the box that I found out. I think it must have been very old stock because the box was brown round the edges, but it turned out that he was a famous film star in the good old days. In his films he often played a sheriff so he always came out on top in the end. I think it must be nice being a sheriff, having a badge and a horse and being able to shoot people without being told off. It's a funny thing, but I often wonder what they did in the evenings. There were lots of pictures inside the box to give you an idea.

To start with, there wasn't a television to be seen, not even in the living room. I suppose they just sat on their horse all day long waiting for something to happen.

He was quick on the draw, though. One moment his six-shooter was in its holster. Then, before you had time to blink, it was pointing straight at the villain as he came round a corner into the main street. After he'd shot people he always blew the smoke away from the end of the barrel, then twirled the gun round his finger several times before putting it back in its holster.

Mind you, John wasn't his real name either. His real name was Marion. I don't blame him for changing it. If you happened to be a sheriff, you would, wouldn't you? You can't have a proper shoot-out with someone if your name's Marion. No one would take you seriously.

Somehow I can't picture Dad as a sheriff. He's more of a nine-to-five person. I don't think he would like being called out in the night to catch some cattle rustlers.

Anyway, my outfit came with a gun that went off bang. It was only caps, of course, but indoors it sounded just like the real thing. It didn't half make people jump when I crept up behind them, especially if they were just nodding off after lunch. It almost got taken away from me that same day. I'd just nearly given my Auntie Beatrice, who was staying with us, a heart attack and I was practising twirling it round like John Wayne did in his films, when it came off my finger and went straight through the dining-room window.

People who mend windows don't half charge a lot for coming out on Christmas Day. I bet if Mum had been married to John Wayne, he wouldn't have spent the whole evening grumbling about the price of things like Dad did.

Auntie Beatrice left soon after dawn on Boxing Day, so Dad took us all out to see some friends of his who live in the next village. He said the fresh air would do us good.

We arrived as they were all going off to church. I liked Dad's friend, but I didn't think much of his wife. She was dressed up to the nines, as though she was going to a wedding. I heard Mum whisper to Dad that she looked like mutton dressed up as lamb, and I could tell she wished she hadn't let me wear my cowboy outfit.

They had a son called Graham who's the same age as me, and funnily enough he'd also been given a gun for Christmas, so he brought it with him and let me play with it. It was one up on mine. Mine's a double-action army Frontier model. His was the Colt single-action army 1873, Sheriff model.

Now, this may not mean much to you, but the difference between single- and double-action guns is that with double action you have to pull the trigger twice – once to cock it and then once more to rotate the cylinder so that you have a bullet lined up in front of the firing pin. All you need to do with an SAA 1873 is pull the trigger once and it sets everything in motion – including firing the bullet.

I must admit I didn't know that myself at the time, although I do now of course, because that was how it came to go off in the middle of the sermon. I was as surprised as anyone.

The whole congregation leaped to its feet; all those who didn't throw themselves on the floor, that is. The vicar crossed himself when he saw the end of the gun pointing towards him over the top of a pew. Well, you've got to take aim at something, or someone; otherwise there's no fun in it.

All the same, I don't think crouching down behind the pulpit is a very good

example of turning the other cheek, which was what he'd just been preaching about. After he had recovered, he changed it to what happens to people who fall victim to temptation and carry guns.

He should talk! When it got near the end of the service, it struck me that he was spending a long time over preparing the bread and the wine; especially the wine. He kept looking over his shoulder to make sure no one was watching.

It was the same with the mince pies on offer as we filed out of the church. I was all for joining in but my Big Sister wasn't having any of it.

'Go away!' she cried in a loud voice as I gave her a nudge. 'I've never seen you before in my life!'

'Fancy letting anyone take a gun into church,' hissed my mum, glaring at

Graham's mum's back.

'Fancy lending it to Harry in the first place,' said Dad, glaring at Graham's back.

'Well, it is Christmas after all,' said Dad's friend, glaring at him.

'Try telling that to the vicar,' said Mum. 'He didn't look as though he was exactly full of good cheer to me. Look at the way he's scowling at all of us now.'

It was while we were going out through the gate that I caught a gleam of metal and spotted a man behind the bushes. I think he may have been after some rabbits. I expect, like everyone else, he was fed up with turkey every year.

'Quick! Down, everyone!' I shouted. 'He's got a gun!'

Well, Mum and Dad and my Big Sister carried on as usual. But their friends –

well, ex-friends really – I've never seen
anyone jump like it. I think it must have
been on account of their being in a nervous
state already. Graham's mum just threw
herself down, and as ill luck would have it,
she landed right in the middle of a puddle.
Gloves . . . hat . . . everything . . . ended up
covered in black mud. Instead of looking
as though she had been to a wedding, she
looked as though she'd spent the night at
a rock concert. It's like I've always said.
There's no point in wearing things that
show the dirt. It's asking for trouble.

'It's you again,' said the vicar as he
bent down to help her up. 'I might have
known!'

Guess what? He wasn't even looking
at her when he said it. He was staring
straight at me. I could smell the wine on
his breath from where I was standing.

'May you be forgiven,' he said, although he didn't sound as if he meant it.

'Excuse me,' I said. 'I think you've spilled something red down the front of your surplice.' They say who laughs last laughs loudest.

The vicar turned to Dad. 'Do you good people live locally?' he asked, between his teeth. 'I don't recall seeing you before.'

'Don't worry,' said Dad. 'You won't be seeing us again in a hurry.'

I've never seen a vicar cheer up so quickly. 'Peace be with you, my son,' he said, laying a hand on my head. 'You should go far.' He didn't actually say the further the better, but I could tell what he was thinking.

'Amen to that,' breathed my Big Sister.

The vicar turned to Mum and Dad. 'We of the cloth should practise what we preach. Tolerance is everything. Let bygones be bygones.'

'I think he's right,' I said as I climbed into the back seat of the car. 'I think everyone ought to be more tolerant. Especially at Christmas.'

And you know what? Nobody, not even Dad, said a word all the way home. I think I might become a vicar when I grow up. Either that or a man who mends windows on Christmas Day.

3

Seeing Stars

Mind you, a cowboy outfit wasn't the only present I had for Christmas; not by a long chalk.

I had a radio-controlled Peugeot rally car set with an extra set of slick tyres and a sprint motor. The only trouble was, I needed four batteries and, would you believe it, there wasn't one in the house.

'Show me something that doesn't need batteries,' groaned Dad. 'Especially on Christmas Day. I think if a mobile electrician selling batteries toured the streets over Christmas he wouldn't have to work again for the rest of the year.'

I bet Max Masters wouldn't have given up that easily. He would have cracked open a piece of stone with a fossilized fish in the middle of it and tapped into a supply of electricity. It beats me how he does it. I once borrowed Dad's hammer and chisel and broke open one of his stones, but I still couldn't see a way in. I suppose the fish must have been very hungry at the time and taken a wrong turning. It was his best rockery stone too!

If you ask me, fish know a lot more than we give them credit for. Take electric eels, for instance. Do you know any human being who can generate his or her own electricity? I asked our science teacher, Miss Jones, whether eels' tails are negative or positive and she suggested I take a meter with me next time I go swimming at the seaside. I don't think she knows really, and she won't let me borrow the school meter. I haven't been allowed anywhere near it since I took the back off during a science lecture. I like finding out how things work. Or don't work, as the case may be. It wasn't my fault the screwdriver slipped.

My Big Sister gave me some handkerchiefs for Christmas, along with some instructions explaining how to use them, and Aunt Beatrice – the one who was staying with us – gave me a drum. It seemed an odd present for someone who doesn't like loud noises. Dad thinks it must have been an afterthought when she realized she hadn't bought me anything. She probably popped into a Tesco on the way.

It certainly wasn't very popular with everyone else, especially as it was made of tin.

It didn't go down too well with Aunt Beatrice either when I tested it outside her bedroom door at six o'clock the next morning. I'd have thought she would be pleased to be woken up by something she'd given me.

Thinking about it, that may be another reason why she left so early.

'Do you think she's got some kind of grudge against us?' asked Dad as we all stood at the front door waving goodbye. 'Something we said, perhaps?'

'Ssh!' said Mum. 'She hasn't even started her car yet. Anyway, we mustn't grumble. At least she's left early. She's got one of her headaches coming on.'

'You can tell she's never had any children,' said Dad.

'I doubt if she ever will now,' said Mum. 'I think she's been put off for life.'

At which point I gave a couple of bangs on the drum, just to make her feel good.

'Don't do that,' said Dad. 'She might never come back.'

It was hard to tell whether he was being serious or not.

'How about opening it up to see where the sound comes from?' broke in my Big Sister, handing me a tin-opener.

'I was thinking I might start a one-man band,' I said, treating the remark with the contempt it deserved. 'Except I can't find my trumpet anywhere. If you play your cards right, I might get you a ticket for *Britain's Got Talent* when I'm on it.'

'If I help you find your trumpet,' she

said, 'will you promise to go off on a nationwide tour straight away?'

Sometimes I think she would make a good Attila the Hun in a school play. Talking of which, did you know he spent his life massacring thousands of people and then he got his come-uppance on his wedding night? If you ask me, he probably married someone like my Big Sister, but he'd been so busy with his massacring he hadn't seen her properly until then. When he woke and saw her close to, he probably died of shock.

That's the sort of thing that makes history come alive. It's the kind of question they don't ask in exams. If they asked that sort of question, I bet I would come out top of the class in history instead of bottom.

But my best present, after the cowboy

outfit, was some-
thing I'd always
wanted: a tele-
scope. And better
still, when I tore
the wrapping
off, it turned
out to be not just
any old telescope,

but a special Astro model. It's got its
own in-built digital computer and it's
called a 'Global Positioning System for
the Universe'.

According to the picture on the side of
the box, once it's been programmed you
can see any object in the sky you want
simply by pressing a button: star clusters,
mountain ranges on the moon, the rings
of Saturn . . . In fact, it's so powerful that
on a clear night it's even possible to home

in on the dust lanes in the Andromeda Galaxy!

Mum got all uptight when I told her on Boxing Day. 'I don't want that around the house for a start,' she said. 'It's bad enough as it is when the sun comes out and shows up all the dust motes. They don't need enlarging.'

'Who knows?' said Dad, taking my side for once. 'If Harry spent more time watching the night sky instead of channel-surfing on the television, he might discover a new star and have it named after him. Then he'd be so famous he'd have no need to form a one-man band.'

'Oh, very romantic!' said my Big Sister, looking up from the mirror I'd given her. Three days she's had it and it hasn't cracked yet – it must be made of steel! 'I mean, brilliant! Imagine being out with a boy and have him look up at the heavens and say, "Do you see what I see? Just to the right of Jupiter. It's that new star everybody's talking about. The one they call Harry." I'd curl up and die with embarrassment on the spot!'

Well, that set my mind working straight away.

'If I do discover a new star,' I said, 'I might get invited on a manned space mission so that I can take a closer look.'

'If you really strike lucky,' said my Big Sister, 'you might discover some primitive form of life when you get there. Some bit of floating ectoplasm you could play conkers with, instead of bothering everyone else. You'd have a lot in common, except you'd be at a disadvantage because it would be a lot more intelligent.'

'You want to watch it,' I said. 'Suppose

I went on a space walk and got hit by a stray meteor. I might get knocked flying and go into permanent orbit. Think of that!'

'Promises, promises,' said my Big Sister, going back to what I call 'Mission Impossible': trying to make her face look better with the box of make-up she'd been given.

After that I went upstairs, taking everything with me. Some people must always have the last word. Besides, I couldn't wait for it to get dark. Have you ever noticed? In the summer when you want it to get dark early, it seems to stay light for ever. Then, in the winter, when you want it to stay light, it seems to get dark before tea time.

Funny thing, though – while I was in my room, having got fed up with trying to open up my drum, I couldn't wait any longer, and before it got really dark I did sort of discover a new star. Well, it wasn't exactly a star, it was more of a heavenly body.

According to the box, with a Global Positioning System you can see more in twenty minutes than Galileo did in a lifetime. I bet I can beat that.

I bet he didn't see what I saw.

I bet Galileo never saw Gloria Braithwaite in her bedroom. Or even Gloria's great-great-great-grandmother in hers, come to that, which I suppose is what could have happened had she been staying in Italy at the time and not bothered to draw the curtains.

I happened to be looking at Gloria's bedroom, not for any particular reason, but simply because it's on the other side of the road from us and in the winter you can see through the trees.

Then, hey presto! There she was, just as though it was meant. Talk about filling the frame. I bet if the manufacturers put a picture of Gloria on the side of the box the Global Positioning System came in, their sales would rocket. I might write to them and suggest it. I could be her agent.

Anyway, I couldn't wait to spread the word. It was too good to keep to myself, especially at Christmas – the so-called season of good will. Besides, what are friends for if you can't share things with them?

I think she must have got some new clothes and make-up for Christmas because she kept posing in front of a large mirror. And not any old posing, she was all 'done up', dancing and singing into a hairbrush as though it was a microphone! She must have thought she was on *Britain's Got Talent*. I nearly dropped the telescope, I was laughing so much.

Luckily Mum and my Big Sister had gone out food shopping and Dad was taking a nap, so I sent out a lot of text messages on his mobile.

By the time I'd finished keying Gloria's exact position into the database, they were all at the door. It being Christmas, everyone was flush with money and they hadn't had a chance to spend it, so at twenty pence a go I couldn't fail, especially

as most of them wanted seconds and even thirds. My best friend, Gordon, had four goes – but then he would. He's like that with chocolate cakes. In no time at all I had three pounds fifty.

It would have been more, except Gloria suddenly spotted us watching her in the mirror and blew her top. I can't say I blame her, but a cheer went up as she started running around the room like a bat

possessed. She was
in such a hurry
she collided with
her stool twice.

Unfortunately
the cheers brought
my dad running to
see what was going
on, and even more
unfortunately he
arrived at our window
at exactly the same moment as Gloria's
mother arrived at hers holding a camera
and took a photograph of everyone at our
window.

'Hyenas!' she called.

So Dad shouldered most of the blame
and no one is speaking to anyone any
more.

Talking of bats reminds me – did you

know that vampire bats don't really suck the blood of their victims like most people think they do? Miss Jones says they simply puncture the skin with their razor-sharp incisors and wait till the blood starts running out, then they lap it up. It's the only thing they can eat without needing indigestion tablets because they don't have a proper stomach, only a long tube.

Another thing about bats is, when they've finished their dinner or whatever they call it in bat language, they don't need a toothbrush. They simply hang upside down on a convenient ledge, like the sort you get under a bathroom mirror. Then they hold on with one foot while they clean their teeth with the other.

I think things like that are interesting.

I must say that for Miss Jones. Apart from knowing all about bats, she does have a lovely set of gnashers. I sometimes wonder if she hangs upside down at night when she goes to bed. If she lived close enough, I might be able to key her into my Global Positioning System as well and find out. I could have asked double rates from all my friends, except it's been confiscated!

'What bothers me,' said Mum, later that day, 'is who's been at my tin-opener while we've been out . . . For some reason it's all bent!'

I tell you, there's never a dull moment in our house.

4

Pets

I think if I was ever lucky enough to have a pet, it wouldn't be a dog or a cat, it would be a pig. The other day Miss Jones was telling us that Sir Winston Churchill, who was our Prime Minister during World War II, once said that whereas dogs look up to us and cats look down on us, pigs treat us as equals.

It must be nice to be treated as an equal. By the sound of it, we would have won the war even sooner if Sir Winston had had a pig alongside him. I bet they would have got on together like a house on fire.

Which reminds me . . . I haven't told you about the time I nearly burned the school down. I was in a play about a plot to blow up the Houses of Parliament and I was given the part of Guy Fawkes.

'Talk about asking for trouble,' said my Big Sister. 'Some people never learn.'

It wasn't much of a part. All I had to do was light a pretend bomb and throw it through one of the windows. Nobody said anything about my using pretend matches as well. Luckily it happened during rehearsals – otherwise it might have been worse.

Do you know what it said in my end-of-term school report that year?

It Wasn't Me

> Harry has a distressing tendency to build up even the most minor of walk-on parts into something approaching a major role. Last year he was given the part of a bumble bee and he kept flying out of the window.

They enclosed a bill for the scenery, but Dad wasn't having any of it. He's good at saying 'No'. Like the time we had a bad meal in a big restaurant: when the bill came, he told them he was giving them what he thought it was worth – no more and no less. It turned out to be a lot less than they had in mind, and they called the police, but the police took one look at what was left on our plates and said they didn't blame him. To make matters worse, everyone else in the restaurant had been listening in and they all started doing the same thing. We haven't been back since. I think Dad's worried about what they might do to anything he orders, especially if it happens to be soup. He might not know until it's too late and he's at death's door.

If you ask me, the fire at the school was worse than it might have been because they didn't have an emergency button.

My great-grandma's got an emergency button and she doesn't even put on plays. It's big and red and she keeps it by the front door just in case. She lives by herself in the country where you meet all sorts of things you don't see in London: owls and sheep and things called peasants. The first time I went to stay with her by myself I went outside to do some exploring and I met a ginormous worm on the front path. That's when I ran back indoors and pressed the button.

It Wasn't Me

I was expecting my great-grandma to come to my rescue. Instead of which I heard bells in the distance. The sound got closer and closer and in the end a fire engine turned up.

My great-grandma couldn't believe it. 'You've only been here five minutes,' she said.

'Twelve,' I said. 'It took the fire engine seven minutes to get here. I timed it.'

I don't think the fire-fighters minded too much. It's what's known as a volunteer fire brigade, which means they all have other jobs. So they got time off work and my great-grandma gave them coffee and cakes.

'You must come again next year,' one of them said to me.

I thought my great-grandma would be cross with me after they left, but all she said was: 'At least we know it works.' And she gave me a wink as though it was a secret between the two of us. She's like that.

Soon after that it was half-term and I went to spend the day with my grandparents. 'When do you go back?' asked Papa, who is really my grandfather

It Wasn't Me

(nicknames run in our family), as he opened the front door.

Grown-ups are like that. Even the best ones. They never say, 'How nice! It's half-term again.' It's always: 'When do you go back?'

Anyway, I was telling them all about how the scenery caught fire.

'I suppose you were nowhere near it at the time,' said Papa.

I know why he said that. It was because soon after I arrived at their house he found the coffee machine switched on. Well, I saw this button sticking out and I couldn't resist it.

'Oh dear, oh dear,' he said. 'I'd better phone the police. I'll tell them we've got this funny fault. The red light on our coffee machine keeps coming on all by itself.'

And he did too. He picked up the telephone and he dialled a number. I hung around looking out of the front window for a police car, but no one turned up. Thinking about it afterwards, I suspect it was only a pretend call.

Papa is always doing things like that. Like the time he explained to me how they make pasteurized milk.

He picked up a milk bottle, passed it in front of me and said, 'There you are. It's been past your eyes.'

I tried it out on our science mistress, Miss Jones, but she didn't seem to think it was at all funny. I suppose it's the way you tell them.

I like staying with my grandparents, and not just because Dad says it's good for them. He says it makes them appreciate what other people have to go through in life.

You can do things with grandparents that you wouldn't be allowed to do at home.

Mind you, they're funny people. Papa has a front doorbell, but he always grumbles if anyone uses it after six o'clock. He says things like, 'Don't go,' and 'Pretend we're not in.'

I think he's frightened it might be someone selling dusters. I don't blame him. Grandma's got a whole cupboard full. Every time she opens the door they all fall out.

It's the same with the telephone when Papa's watching *EastEnders*. 'Who's that ringing up at this time of night?' he says. 'Pretend we're out.'

Papa often says, give me five minutes in his house and NOTHING works. He says by the time I've been there for a day he has to get all his manuals out to make everything work again.

He also says certain key words affect me. Words like: WET PAINT; DANGER – KEEP OUT; KEEP OFF THE GRASS and DON'T TOUCH; especially DON'T TOUCH.

I have to admit he's right about the last one. I think it's asking for trouble. If they put something like TOUCH THIS AS MUCH AS YOU LIKE, they wouldn't have anything to worry about.

I'll give you an example. The other day Sue (I call Grandma Sue because she said I could) was baking some cakes. When she took them out of the oven, she turned to me and said: 'They're hot, Harry.

Whatever you do, don't touch them.'

So of course I did –
I mean, what did she
expect? It so happened
the one I poked my
finger into was RED
HOT. And do you
know what? I didn't
get any sympathy. She
said it served me right and

Papa said he hoped it wasn't his cake
because he'd been looking forward to it;
it was a good job I didn't work in a bakery
because a cake fresh out of the oven is a
bit like the world – the further inside you
go, the hotter it gets. Which was not what
I wanted to hear at all. Anyway, who
would want to poke their finger inside the
world? Apart from being made to clean
your nails for days afterwards, you'd need

a ginormously long one to reach right into the middle. It's over 6,000 kilometres deep at the equator.

As it was, it's lucky for them my finger didn't melt. They would have been really sorry if it had and I'd been left with only four. I said Mum and Dad wouldn't let me go to stay with them ever again if that had happened, but it didn't seem to worry them. All the same, I expect it has put them off home-made cakes for ever after, because it will always remind them of what might have happened.

'It isn't fair,' I said.

'Well, at least you've learned something today,' said Papa as Sue dipped my finger in cold water and then put a bandage on it. 'Life isn't fair from the moment you're born. You have to ride over these things,'

After that I thought perhaps I might

earn some Brownie points by helping Sue with some more cakes she was making.

The trouble with chocolate cakes, especially if you are standing on a chair, is that if you happen to switch the mixer on before you put the top on, you get brown splodges all over the wall. I think they ought to invent a mixer which can't do that. If they can put a man on the moon, they ought to be able to do something simple like fit some kind of chocolate mix sensor on a kitchen mixer. Either that or people should only make cakes that match the colour of their walls.

I like helping in the kitchen. For some reason I'm not allowed to at home. The last time I joined in I caught Mum kicking the fridge when she thought I wasn't looking. She broke her toe, and it didn't do the fridge door a lot of good. Looking

at her, you would think butter wouldn't melt in her mouth and she would never do a thing like that, but you never know with grown-ups. One moment they're all sweetness and light, the next it's a case of running for cover.

It Wasn't Me

You can tell what sort of mood Papa is in by the kind of songs he sings. The other day I heard him singing something like '*An apple for the teacher, to show I'm meek and mild, and that I really am not just a problem child. You're going to get all my affection, your wish will be my rule . . .*'

I know what would happen if I gave an apple to my teacher. She'd send it to an analyst to make sure it hadn't been poisoned.

Sometimes when I'm staying with them, Papa sings things like 'Many Brave Hearts Are Asleep in the Deep' and I know that means trouble. One day when I could see he was feeling a bit down, I offered to make him a risotto. I even wrote out the recipe for him. It was one I'd come across in a book.

1 onion
About 6 sausages
1 cup of rice
Palmerston cheese
1 teespone thyme

'I hope it tastes better than it spells,' said Papa.

'Don't you mean smells?' I said.

'I know what I mean,' said Papa, and he fell about laughing. He quite often laughs at his own jokes. Sometimes he's the only person who does. But at least the thought had cheered him up.

In the end I didn't make it because Sue didn't have the right kind of cheese. She only had Gruyere. I always called it Grulio. One day Mum went into a famous cheese shop and by mistake asked for 250 grams of Grulio.

'I'm afraid we're out of it at the moment,' said the man. 'We're expecting some in any day.'

Afterwards Mum said it was very nice of him because she could tell he didn't want her to feel embarrassed in front of all the other customers, but I don't think he knew what he was talking about. As we left, I saw him looking in a book.

'Never mind,' said Papa when he came in from the garden. 'Sue hasn't got the cheese and I don't have the thyme. Anyway there's nothing that two days in a darkened room won't cure.' Once again he started laughing.

It was while Sue was scrubbing the wall to get rid of the chocolate stains that I heard her say something that set me thinking. 'What Harry needs,' she said, 'is some kind of pet.'

'A piranha fish?' suggested Papa. 'Preferably one that hasn't been fed for a long time. He could play with it in the bath.'

'At least he wouldn't be able to put his finger in the water,' said Sue. 'But I'm being serious. He needs something to keep his mind occupied.'

Which is really how I came to meet Mortimer. That, and Mum's new car. I think in a strange kind of way the two coming together must have been meant.

That's one of the nice things about Papa. He understands what children like and I told him so.

'You're as old as you feel,' he announced.

I asked him how old he felt.

'A hundred and five,' he said as he waved goodbye.

5

A Strange Sighting

You're probably wondering what Mum getting a new car had to do with my getting a pig. Well, it all came about because she couldn't wait to take us out for a drive and we got lost.

Have you ever noticed how grown-ups often have disagreements when they're together in a car? Get them sitting behind a wheel, or even alongside it, and they become different people. And another thing: it's almost always the one who isn't driving who sets it off.

If it was a competition, my dad would win hands down. He's got it down to a fine art. He waits until exactly the right moment, like when Mum's going round Hyde Park Corner during the evening rush hour. Then he says, 'Why are you still in third?'

I bet whoever invented the automatic gear box did it because he couldn't stand the way his partner drove when she went round Hyde Park Corner. Dad says you should never catch anyone else's eye, but Mum's always waving to people and letting them go first, which they all do, of course. It takes us ages to get round sometimes.

Another favourite ploy of Dad's is when Mum suddenly asks which exit she needs to take at the next roundabout. (I think

he keeps it for when we're in the country
– preferably on a bank holiday.)

He comes up with something simple
like: 'The one heading north.'

Mum always takes the bait and says:
'Which way is north?'

That does it. Dad gives a snort and
gets going with things like: 'It's a good job
you're not in charge of a polar expedition.
Imagine all those huskies trying to pull
a sledge along the front at Brighton on a

Saturday afternoon in August.'

By then we've been round the round-about twice and are heading back the way we came.

After that he starts making sucking noises through his teeth and saying: 'That was a narrow squeak!' Then if Mum says, 'But there was no one else around,' he comes back with: 'I was talking about the kerb.'

Then there's parking. Mum only needs to say, 'Where shall we park?' and he comes out with: 'Well, you're driving.' Then he washes his hands of the whole thing and starts fiddling with the radio to see if there's anything more interesting to listen to while she makes up her mind.

The thing is, it takes a while because Mum isn't very good at getting into small spaces so she usually drives around looking for what she calls 'a suitable gap'. Then, when she finds one, that sets Dad off again: 'Lucky you got the last three spaces,' and 'Which meter would you like me to feed – the one up the road or the one you've just hit with the back bumper?'

It's funny how two people can live together for years and yet still not know the simplest things about each other. Like my Uncle Ernest and Auntie Mamie. They've had a car all their lives – something called a Morris Oxford. Uncle Ernest always says they don't make cars like that these days. I won't tell you what Dad says.

Anyway, I don't think they had ever been out in it after dark on account of Auntie Mamie not seeing too well. Then one day they lost their way and found themselves in a tunnel. It was a long one, and by the time they came out the other end they weren't speaking to each other, which wasn't surprising because everyone who saw them afterwards said they were like two different people.

Soon after that they sold the car.

I think when people get married they ought to fill in questionnaires. Like the sort my dad sometimes gets, with lots of little boxes to tick. (They usually say this will only take a few minutes of your time, but he gets cross because it takes him all evening and he wishes he'd never started.) The other thing about them is they say things like: the sender of the first one to be opened will receive a gift, but he's never got anything yet.

All it would need is some simple questions about things every couple ought to know. Questions like: 'Do you know where the light switch is on your car? Do either of you suffer from claustrophobia? Fear of the dark? Oncoming headlights?'

In Auntie Mamie's case it would have been one cross for 'No', followed by three ticks, but Uncle Ernest didn't know that until they were in the tunnel and it was too late.

I was thinking about all that, and people in general, when I suddenly came to and realized that Mum and Dad were talking to each other through gritted teeth, which is usually a bad sign, especially when they start calling each other 'dear'.

When you come to think about it, 'gritting your teeth' is a funny expression. I mean, they grit roads to stop cars skidding when it's icy, but teeth! I suppose it's to stop them skidding when they come together on all that saliva.

Nature's interesting that way. I'll tell you something about saliva. According to Miss Jones, it's got a chemical in it that's good for healing wounds. That's why some people, especially mothers, say things like 'Let me kiss it better' when you fall over on your roller skates. I wouldn't fancy kissing my Big Sister's knees better, but that makes two of us. It's also supposed to be good for cleaning things – which is how the saying 'spit and polish' came about.

Going back to teeth, I think my great-grandpa had the right idea. He used to take his teeth out at night, which must have been very useful. He never had to have them filled, and he never, ever had toothache. I don't know why they did away with false teeth. I asked my dentist and he said he

could arrange some for me on the spot. Then I wouldn't need to visit him again. But that was after I'd broken his chair. It served him right for leaving me alone with it. I was trying to see how high I could make it go and it got jammed. I suppose he didn't like having to stand on a box.

I asked Miss Jones about that too, and she said they probably did away with false teeth so that dentists could get even richer. She says that plug-in teeth may be the next thing. She says we live in an age when nothing gets repaired, it just gets replaced, and that human beings may be like that one day. You'll be able to go into a shop and buy a new plug-in arm or liver.

She also told us that the average fully grown human generates 1.5 litres of saliva every twenty-four hours. I don't know how they measured it unless they got someone to go around drooling into a glass all day, but who's to argue? I reckon my dad must have got through about five litres the day we got lost.

'Name me just one famous woman navigator, dear,' he was saying.

'Amy Johnson, dear,' said Mum, quick as a flash. 'She flew all the way from Croydon to Australia by herself in just over nineteen days.'

'She probably only wanted to go to Guildford,' said Dad.

After that no one said anything for a while. 'Anyway,' said Dad, in the kind of voice he uses to show he was right all the time, 'what kept her? I mean, nineteen days. A man would have done it in a tenth of the time.'

'Not in 1930 they wouldn't have,' said Mum.

It was at that point that she suggested he drive the car. It was either that or we all walked home and left it in the lay-by she had turned into by mistake.

After that all was quiet again for a bit until Dad suddenly said: 'Where are we?'

'You're driving,' said Mum, getting her own back. 'You should know.'

'You've got the road atlas, dear,' said Dad. gritting his teeth again. 'Haven't you been following the route?'

Well, it went to and fro like that for a while and I didn't take much notice until I suddenly realized Dad was talking to me.

'How about you having a go, Harry?' he said. 'You know all about Global Positioning. See what you can do with this.' And he thrust a great book into my arms.

'Easy peasy,' I said. 'Leave it to me. Where are we?'

'What do you mean where are we?' said Dad. 'That's what I'm asking you.'

Well, I mean . . . What's the point of having a book of road maps if it doesn't tell you where you are?

'I can see a signpost saying "Mortimer three miles",' said Mum, looking out of the window.

'There you are,' said Dad. 'All you've got to do is look for Mortimer on the map and we're home and dry.'

Well, that was all very well, but I soon discovered another thing about maps.

It doesn't matter what place you want to look up, it's always on a join. I found Mort, but when I looked for an imer to join on the end, I couldn't see it anywhere. Then I discovered that although I'd been

on page 14, the
next bit of the
map was on page
72 because it had
started off again
on the other side
of England.

'It's no wonder
people go off on expeditions and never get
heard of again,' I said.

'When was the last time you heard of
anyone going off on an expedition and
disappearing off the face of the earth?'
said Dad.

That set my Big Sister off. Up
until then she'd been sitting in the
back trying to paint stars on her
fingernails – which isn't easy when Dad's
driving and he's in a bad mood, I can
tell you.

'I can think of a good candidate right now,' she said pointedly.

I looked out of the window in case there was another signpost I could try, and that was when I saw them: a girl with what looked like a small black and white dog waddling along after her on the end of a lead. Except that it wasn't a dog. It had a flat black nose at one end, more of a snout really, a tiny curly tail at the other, and a leg at all four corners.

'Did you see that?' I cried. 'Did you see that? It looked just like a pig going for a walk.'

'Brilliant,' said my Big Sister, using her know-all voice. 'Ten out of ten. It was a miniature Chinese pot-bellied pig. You don't see many of those about. Despite the fact that they've been domesticated ever since the tenth century.'

'The first book about them was written over five thousand years ago,' agreed Dad, taking his eyes off the road for a moment.

Suddenly everything fell into place. I knew what I wanted most of all in my life. Even more than a new skateboard. I even knew what I would call it if I had one. I think names are important, especially if you're a pig and don't have very much else.

'If I had a pig like that,' I said, 'I'd call it Mortimer.'

'You're not having one,' said Mum, reading my thoughts. 'I can tell you that for a start. Besides, where would it do its whatsits?'

'Its "whatsits"?' I repeated. 'What are "whatsits"?'

There was a groan from my Big Sister. 'You'd find out soon enough if you had to clear up after it.'

'I know who'd end up doing that,' said Mum. 'It would be like Harold the hamster all over again.'

'Hamsters are boring,' I said. 'They don't do anything except go round and round on their wheel all day. Harold never did anything interesting like going for walks on a lead.'

After that I couldn't wait to go home. As soon as we got indoors I added 'Chinese pot-bellied pig' to my birthday list. I left it lying around for days, but nobody said anything.

Then, after my birthday had been and gone and there was still no sign of one, I decided to take matters into my own hands, and one day I settled down to start thinking it through.

My Big Sister noticed it first. 'You want to watch out,' she said. 'All that brainwork just after breakfast. You'll do yourself a mischief. Anyway,' she demanded when she could see I wasn't listening, 'if you got a pot-bellied pig, what would you feed it on?'

'He can share my Mars bars,' I said. 'Boiled sweets. Odd scraps. Anything I can get hold of.'

She gave a sniff. 'You want to think again,' she said. 'They're not like ordinary pigs. If you don't believe me, go and get a book out of the library. Better still, get him a library ticket, then he can do it himself. You'll only make a mess of it!'

You wait, I thought. *Just you wait!*

6

Wishing Will Make It So

Have you ever tried getting a book on miniature Chinese pot-bellied pigs at your local library? It's worse than trying to get through to Fort Knox. I should know. I've tried both.

I expect you're wondering why I wanted to phone Fort Knox. Well, it was to do with a bet I had with Gordon. It all started when I said that I could see inside anywhere in the world with my Global Positioning System. All I had to do was key in its exact position on the map. He said I couldn't because it didn't see round corners, and because the world was round and America was over three thousand miles away it wouldn't be possible anyway.

I said, 'The trouble with you, Gordon, is you believe everything you're told.'

So he said: 'All right then, show me the inside of Fort Knox.' We were doing American history at the time, which I chose because they haven't got very much. Not like us. (I think we've got far too much.)

I had to give up in the end. I don't think anyone in Fort Knox knew where they were, or if they did they weren't letting on. When I phoned them, they kept telling me to hang on. And that's another thing. What I didn't know at the time was that nowadays when the telephone bill comes in, it lists all the numbers that have been dialled. I'd rung Fort Knox so many times, Dad got a note asking if we would like to add the number to our list of calls for what they call CHEAP RATES.

You should have seen his face at breakfast when he read it. He couldn't believe his eyes. He jabbed so hard with his teaspoon, it went right through the bottom of his boiled egg!

Anyway, back to Mortimer. Like my Big Sister suggested, first of all I tried the public library. I managed to get out during the school lunch hour. The best thing about that was, I won Brownie points because I asked for permission. Which only goes to show there's good in everything. After that it was downhill all the way.

Mistake number one was telling the man at the desk that my Big Sister told me he was the best person to come to if I wanted to learn all about pot-bellied pigs on account of the fact that he looked like one.

If you think my dad was cross when he heard about my telephone calls to Fort Knox, he had nothing on the man at the library. I've heard of road rage, but his was ten times worse. You'd think with a name like 'public library' they'd be glad when people came in asking them things.

It Wasn't Me

I must say, looking back on it, he did have a face that was rather like a pig. Luckily I didn't give up. School seemed to last for ever that day, but as soon as the bell went, I rushed out and went straight back to the library. This time there was a girl behind the counter. She recognized me straight away.

'If you want the latest Max Masters,' she said, 'you're out of luck. It's set in France and it's all about the Eiffel Tower. There's been a run on it, with the Easter holidays coming up.'

So I decided to try a different tack. Looking over my shoulder in case her boss overheard, I said I was wanting a book for a friend.

'He'll need a ticket,' she said. 'I'll give you a form for him to sign. Is he a rate-payer?'

I nearly gave the game away by saying that pigs didn't pay rates, but I stopped myself just in time. 'I don't think he's old enough,' I said.

'Do you know his date of birth?' she asked.

That was an even harder question to answer.

'Nobody knows,' I said. Well, I wasn't going to say it was me all the time.

'Oh dear,' she said. 'That's not a very good start in life. Does he have a name?'

'Mortimer,' I said. 'Mortimer Manners.'

'Mortimer Manners,' repeated the girl. 'That's very alliterative.'

'I don't suppose he's ever been to school,' I said.

She gave me a funny look at that point and explained that alliterative didn't mean he couldn't read or write, it meant having words beginning with the same letter.

You learn something new every day.

'It's too late to change it now,' I said. 'The thing is, he's not very good at reading, so I promised I would look some things up for him.'

It was the girl's turn to glance over her shoulder. 'Why don't you find what you want,' she said. 'Then bring it to me and I'll make some copies for him.'

Which is what I ended up doing. It took me a long time because I didn't know where to start, but in the end I found a book on pot-bellied pigs in a tiny section called 'Pets (Exotic)'. I don't think anyone had ever had it out before because it looked all new and shiny and there were no dates stamped inside to say it should have been returned three weeks ago, like there usually are in my Big Sister's books.

But I found out all I wanted to know. It was all down in black and white. As you might expect, pot-bellied pigs don't really mind what they eat, but for a treat they like grapes and sliced apple. In fact, they're keen on most kinds of fruit, especially avocados and bananas.

They also like unsalted popcorn – which is good news because I like that too. I might take Mortimer to the cinema next time I go. But they shouldn't eat tomatoes or green peppers. Rhubarb plants are poisonous to them, and unlike the nursery rhyme, the little piggy who didn't have roast beef was better off than the one who did. And did you know that as well as being brushed regularly, they also need oiling? Not with an oil can, as you might think, but with lotion rubbed into the skin.

It was while I was looking through some pictures at the back of the book that it suddenly came to me why they looked so familiar.

I waited while the girl copied the pages for me. Then, after she'd promised to save the Max Masters for me, I dashed out again and made my way to a shop I knew. I must have passed it a trillion times on my way to and from school, and once or twice I'd stopped to look in the window, but I'd never plucked up the courage to go inside.

It's called Oddments, and for as long as I can remember it's been closing down. The sign outside saying EVERYTHING MUST GO looks older than the shop.

If you ask me, I think it must have

been meant, because I knew that this was where I'd once seen a pig just like the ones in the pictures. I ran the last part of the way because I was frightened it might have gone, but luckily it was still there, sitting on top of a box sandwiched between a painting of an old  lady doing her knitting and a large vase.

'The Chinese pig?' The man seemed surprised. 'It's your lucky day, son,' he said gravely. 'There've been lots of enquiries about him because he comes fully housetrained. He's only been hanging fire on account of being difficult to gift wrap. It's the legs, you know.' He looked me up and down. 'How much were you thinking of paying?'

'How much were you thinking of asking?' I said, taking a leaf out of Dad's book. 'I haven't got very much money.'

'I'm not asking two pounds for it,' he said. 'I'm not even asking one. He's yours for fifty p.'

Luckily I had my savings left over from the Gloria episode with me so I was able to pay: he had it inside a carrier bag before I had time to open my mouth.

'And no bringing it back,' he shouted after me. 'We don't do refunds.'

But I didn't mind. He was just what I wanted. Until that moment Mortimer had always been a pretend pet; now that I had one for real, I wouldn't swap him for all the tea in China – except that would be like sending coals to Newcastle seeing as that's where they come from.

He's got big round eyes – not like an

ordinary pig's – and his skin feels as though it's made of the softest leather. It's mostly black and he's got a leg at each corner; exactly like the one I saw when we were out for the drive.

As soon as I got home I took Mortimer upstairs so that I could show him a view of the back garden from the spare-room window. From there you can look down on the patio and see beyond the pergola to the lawn and the flowerbeds beyond. Luckily it's what they call a walled garden, so he's not likely to get lost. I pointed out where he could go and where he couldn't. Mum's very keen on her flowers and she hates it when plants get trampled on.

Then, seeing as my Big Sister wasn't home from school yet, I went into her room and picked up a couple of things Mortimer might need. Then I showed him the bathroom, and after that we went back to my bedroom.

I opened up the drawer where I thought he might like to sleep at night, and showed him the trunk where I keep my bits and pieces. Looking around the room, he seemed to like the wallpaper best. I know what he means. It's got lots of flowers all over it. I don't know what sort they are, but they're very good for counting in the summer when it stays light late at night and I can't get to sleep. I once reached two thousand and seventy-three and I was wide awake by then.

I showed him the view across the road, but there was no sign of Gloria Braithwaite. I wasn't surprised because I haven't seen her for ages. She keeps her curtains tightly drawn these days. I told Mortimer he wasn't missing very much.

Luckily he kept very quiet and didn't give the game away by grunting or snorting or squealing like pigs often do. I bet he would have squealed if he had seen Gloria.

'If you ask me, Mortimer,' I said as I laid him in the drawer, 'it's a good job I went to the library. We would never have met up otherwise.'

I must say he looked nice and cosy tucked up in the chest of drawers. I knew how he felt. There's something special about hay when you're lying back in it with your legs in the air. I think it has a lot to do with the smell. I left the drawer slightly open so that he could breathe properly. I expect pot-bellied pigs snore if they can't breathe.

Just then the door opened and my Big Sister came into the bedroom. 'Talking to yourself again?' she said. Then she glanced at the floor. 'So that's where my hairbrush went to. And my best body lotion!'

'Ssh,' I said, before I could stop myself. 'You'll wake Mortimer.'

'Mortimer?' She treated me to one of her pitying looks. 'You know what your trouble is? I've said it before and I'll say it again: you live in a dream world.' And with that she slammed the door shut.

Well, that did it. 'Some people,' I shouted after her, 'don't have any imagination!' And that was the last thing we said to each other for several days. I was going to show her Mortimer, but I decided not to. I'd keep him a secret from everyone. I feel sorry for people who don't have dreams. Mortimer was the best pig in the whole wide world.

As I returned to rubbing his back with what was left of my Big Sister's body lotion, I thought of another good thing about him. Mum was never likely to have any trouble with his whatsits!

7

Springtime in Paris

I knew it wasn't a good start to the day when Dad got locked in the lavatory just as we were about to leave home, and we had another upset at St Pancras station.

We were on our way to catch the Eurostar to Paris for a few days, and after we passed through security Mum, my Big Sister and I had gone quite a way before we realized Dad wasn't with us any more.

Mum was the first to notice.

'Where's your father?' she said, looking over her shoulder.

We retraced our steps, and you'll never guess what we saw. He was with a lot of men in uniform and they were all looking at MY COWBOY GUN. I had been wondering where it was. It turned

out that Mum had forgotten she'd hidden it in one of their suitcases soon after it was taken away from me at Christmas, and it had showed up on the screen. Even though it wasn't a real one, they were lecturing Dad for setting a bad example to children.

'What a place to put it!' he cried as we drew near.

'Well, you told me to hide it somewhere safe,' said Mum. 'It seemed as good a place as any. Besides, you packed the case. Didn't you look in all the pockets?'

Dad couldn't think of a suitable answer, so everybody turned to look at me as though it was my fault.

Once grown-ups get hold of something like that, it feels as though you're never going to hear the end of it. They were still talking about it an hour later when we were on the train. As it happened, it was Dad who changed the subject, much to my relief.

'We are about to enter the tunnel,' he said. 'If you look out of the window, you may see some fish going past.' That's the kind of thing my grandfather says.

I ignored him and turned instead to the new Max Masters book I'd got from the library. Dad said he hoped it would keep me quiet, but in the end it kept everybody quiet except for me. I had to speak loud because of the noise.

'Did you know,' I shouted, 'that when they built the tunnel, they had to remove nearly eight million cubic metres of earth? Think of the ginormous hole it must have left. It's a wonder the roof doesn't fall in with nothing left to support it. I bet the water wouldn't half rush in if it sprang a leak. I expect that's why the trains go so fast. They want to reach the other end before it collapses. If it did, there'd be no escape.'

It Wasn't Me

That did the trick. Mum and Dad stopped talking. In fact, everyone in the carriage stopped talking.

'I do wish you'd keep your voice down,' whispered Mum.

'I suppose if the water came in ahead of us, the driver could try putting the train into reverse,' I shouted, trying to make everybody feel better. 'Of course, he'd have to stop first – otherwise he would damage the gears, and then we'd really be stuck.'

'Do you mind?' said my Big Sister.

'I hope the Mafia weren't involved with any of the firms who did the concreting,' I continued. 'They might have buried lots of bodies in the wet cement. My friend Barry's father said they're supposed to have done that when the overhead road to London airport was being built. He should know, he's a policeman. He says the Chiswick flyover is reckoned to be the worst spot. He always gives it a miss. As the bodies decompose, it leaves a hole in the concrete. I bet there are lots of thin bits in this tunnel.'

'Barry's father ought to know better,' said Mum.

'The boy's got to learn,' said Dad, coming to my rescue for once.

'Yes, but at least he could keep it to himself.'

'Can I do some exploring?' I asked. 'I think Mortimer might get taken short if I stay here too long.'

Everyone seemed to think that was a good idea.

'I don't see why not,' said Dad. 'You can't open the doors while the train's in motion.'

'More's the pity . . .' My Big Sister's voice followed me up the aisle. 'What's the betting he has a go?'

Actually, I didn't get very far, because the first thing I came across was the toilet. Have you ever been in one on Eurostar? It's the best part of the train. What they call 'all mod cons'. I could have stayed in there all day. In fact, I very nearly did, but in the end I got fed up with people knocking on the door.

I couldn't wait to tell the others. 'It's the best toilet I've ever been in,' I said. 'You should have a go. I bet even Dad wouldn't get locked in.'

'Are we nearly there yet?' asked Mum.

You know, that's another thing that's unfair about life. Grown-ups are allowed to ask questions like that, but you try asking it if you're young! I like reading up about things before I go on trips. Someone once said that it's better to travel hopefully than to arrive, and I know what they meant. Not that you could say that about the Eiffel Tower. That was the first thing I looked for when we reached Paris. It was just as Max Masters described it.

I don't think Mum and Dad really wanted to go up to the top. Whenever I caught sight of it they immediately starting pointing at things in the opposite direction. But the thing about the Eiffel Tower is it's so big it won't go away. Everywhere you go you catch glimpses of it. Sometimes when you least expect it. You turn a corner and – *Wham! Bang!* – it's right in front of you. So in the end they gave way.

I kept Mortimer under my jacket as we joined the queue because Dad might have been charged extra for him and it was bad enough as it was. Also I wanted to consult my book.

'It's funny really,' I said as we entered the lift to take us up to the first level. 'When it was first built in 1899, it was only expected to last twenty years. And yet it's still here. That means . . .' I started to count, but even allowing ten years for every finger I only just made it.

'That means,' I said, 'it's over ninety years past its sell-by date. I think they ought to paint that on the side to warn people that it might collapse at any moment.'

'I don't want to know,' said Mum. Funny thing, she had her eyes closed. I don't think she likes heights for some reason.

'I wonder if they're the original cables on the lifts,' I said, thinking out loud. I don't know about you, but I find it difficult not to think out loud about things. 'I mean, I can understand iron lasting all that time, but Max Masters reckons the cables would start to fray with all the wear and tear they suffer from people going up and down, day in, day out.'

'Ssh!' said Mum.

However, it was too late. The lift was packed and it was just like in the train. Everyone had gone quiet.

It Wasn't Me

'It's not as if there's one long lift,' I said, trying to make amends. 'There's two. The second one goes to the platforms above us. At the most we would only fall five hundred and twenty-two feet. Besides, it must be worse in the summer. When it's hot the metal expands and the tower is fifteen centimetres taller.

'I bet you didn't know that,' I called to my Big Sister, who was trying to pretend she was with someone else. 'And another thing. When there's a strong wind, the top can sway as much as twelve centimetres.'

Sometimes you might just as well talk to yourself for all the interest people take. One good thing about the Eiffel Tower: the queues may look big when you first get there, but they soon thin out. By the time we were in the second lift there weren't very many passengers left, which was a good thing because we got a better view of all the rivets holding everything together.

'Do you realize,' I said, 'there are over two and a half million of them? Max Masters reckons they must be suffering metal fatigue by now. I expect if you look closely, a lot of them are about to go pop. He reckons the whole thing is probably held together by paint. It takes over fifty tons to cover the lot, and they do it every seven years. He thinks it's to cover up the cracks.'

I like knowing about things like that. It makes life more interesting.

'If you ask me, he sounds like a Francophobe,' said Dad, breaking the silence.

'I think he's American,' I said. 'He comes from Wisconsin.'

When we stopped at the third level, the other passengers left us to it, which was probably just as well because there are no stairs after that, so the only way back down is by lift.

'At least it means we've got the top of the tower to ourselves,' said Dad. 'Come and have a look at the view. I expect you can see our hotel on a clear day.'

All I could see was heat haze, but I didn't want to disappoint him. Not after it had cost him so much to take us all up.

'It's all right,' I said. 'Can we go back down now?'

Grown-ups are funny about that kind of thing too. It's hard to get things right with them at times.

When we were up the Eiffel Tower, I was in trouble for not looking down at the view. Then, when we got back down again and were walking around looking for somewhere to have lunch, I was in trouble for not looking up.

'I bring you all this way,' said Dad, 'and what happens? All you do is mooch along looking at your feet. You can see those any day of the week. Look at all those beautiful buildings. All that fine architecture . . .'

Then he went all quiet.

'Where's your father?' said Mum. 'Don't tell me he's disappeared again.'

You'll never guess the next bit. Why Dad wasn't there, I mean. It was because he'd fallen down a hole in the pavement, that's why! Have you noticed that things often go in threes? Luckily he landed on a workman. Well, it was lucky for Dad. The workman didn't seem too pleased, especially as he was operating a pneumatic drill at the time.

Dad kept on shouting, '*Pardonnez-moi*,' but we never did find out what the workman said in return 'cause he was talking so fast and waving his arms about as though he'd gone through a wasp's nest with his drill.

Mum thought she heard him say, 'Rule Britannia!' at one point, but she might have got it wrong, what with the noise of the traffic and everything.

'You've got the phrase book,' she said, turning to me. 'See what it says.'

Now, it's a funny thing with phrase books. They never ask the sort of questions you want them to.

I wouldn't like to go on holiday with the man who wrote ours. He sounds like a real wet blanket. Even worse than Dad.

It Wasn't Me

Nothing seems to go right. When he goes to the dentist, he says things like: 'You have removed the wrong tooth!' and when he goes to the seaside there's a picture of him shouting, 'My wife has been swept out to sea!' followed by: 'She can't swim!'

But I couldn't find anything like 'My dad has fallen down a hole in the *trottoir*' (that's French for pavement). I bet he didn't think of that one. Perhaps he didn't have a father to fall down a hole so it didn't occur to him that anyone might need the phrase.

The nearest I got was: '*Est-ce un terrain de golf de dix-huit trous?*' which means: 'Is this an eighteen-hole golf course?' I don't think it went down too well with the workmen.

I called down to Dad. 'Have you broken your leg?' I asked hopefully.

'I don't think so!' he shouted.

'That's a pity,' I said. 'If you had and there were bones sticking out through the skin, I could tell you what to say.'

After that it went quiet until the ambulance arrived. The paramedics were very good. In no time at all they'd put Dad's right arm in a sling, strapped his two legs together, and had him on a stretcher.

It Wasn't Me

I borrowed Mum's digital camera and took a photo of him being lifted into the back of the ambulance. I think I might send it to the school magazine. They're always on the lookout for good action shots.

'You go and enjoy yourselves,' called Dad, putting a brave face on things.

'Certainly not,' said Mum.

'Please,' he said, waving farewell with his good hand. 'I insist.' He even managed a smile. 'I'm perfectly happy by myself.'

'That's typical of your father,' said Mum as the ambulance doors closed. 'Always thinking of others, never himself.'

After they had taken Dad away, we went for a meal and I was in trouble again, only this time it was from Mum. She started grumbling because I was taking a long time eating my chips. I like putting them on top of each other to see how high I can go before they all fall over.

Luckily for me the waiter overheard and he came to my rescue. '*Le jeune homme* is right,' he said. '*Absolument!* The French fries in this establishment are noted for being the best in Paris; possibly in the whole of France – and that means the world! They should be treated with respect and savoured slowly. I will bring him some more.'

You wouldn't catch an English waiter saying that. He'd be more likely to take your plate away the moment you put your knife and fork down for a rest.

I learned something else that day too. It has to do with ordering a drink. In England, if you want to order one of anything and the waiter doesn't understand, you hold up your first finger, meaning one. In France they hold up their thumb for one, so holding up your first finger means you would like two. Which is how I came to get two giant glasses of Coca-Cola.

I think I might come and live in France when I'm older.

8

A Day in the Garden

Now if you think the Eiffel Tower is fab (which it is), wait until you try the Jardin d'Acclimatation.

Everything in Paris seems to be big. For example, it takes for ever to get across the Place de la Concorde and the bus drivers seem to take a delight in driving straight at you. But that's nothing compared to what is known as the Louvre. I was dying to visit one myself at the time, but you should have seen the size of the queue outside.

Well, I thought that's what it was for, but it turned out to be a museum, so it cost Mum a bomb. While we were there we saw a picture of someone called Mona Lisa.

She looked as though she felt like I did before we found the loo!

But the biggest and best thing we came across in Paris was the Jardin d'Acclimatation. It even has its own miniature railway, with a real policeman to stop the traffic every time the train has to cross a road on the way in. Mum said, 'Say what you like about the French, but they do have their priorities right.'

Inside the garden they've got everything. You name it, they've got it. My favourite was a ride on a miniature aeroplane. I was in my element. With my eyes closed I could see it all. Max Masters would have been proud of me.

The pilot was just like Captain X in *Galaxy* (that's a magazine about space travel I get every week). He was a man of few words. Well, he was afterwards. He wasn't at the time. Not when he found himself locked in the lavatory at 20,000 feet. I'd never heard so much swearing before. Not even from Dad when the same thing happened just before we left home to catch the Eurostar, and that had been at ground level. Well, on the top deck, of course!

It's different when you're flying over the Atlantic . . .

Even then it might not have been so bad, but then the co-pilot suffered a blackout because the  nose of the plane suddenly went up, which meant we were going into a stall, and I had to take over the controls.

'That's all right,' I said afterwards. 'Glad to be of help.'

'It's a good job you knew what to do,' said a man who'd been listening to my story. 'I flew Concorde regularly in the good old days, but I didn't realize it was possible to do such a tight turn at over twice the speed of sound. It's lucky the wings didn't fall off.'

'It's lucky I was sitting near the flight deck,' I said simply.

There was a round of applause from the rest of the passengers as I made my way back to the main cabin. I waved it aside, but as I did so I stopped to give the kiss of life to a couple of passengers who'd fainted clean away. Well, only one, actually – because just as I was about to start on the second the money ran out and the plane juddered to a halt.

'Can I have another go, Mum?' I asked.

'It's may I have another go, please,' said Mum. 'And no you can't.'

'How about the Hall of Mirrors?' I said.

That was my second favourite, especially when I found one which made my Big Sister look all short and fat when she stood in front of it. I couldn't stop laughing. She got upset when I pretended I couldn't see any difference, which

made it seem twice as funny, especially when she couldn't find her way out on account of it being a maze as well. I thought it was very good value.

'I think it's high time we collected your father from the hospital,' said Mum. 'They said they were only going to keep him in under observation for one night.'

'It's a good job it didn't happen to Harry,' said my Big Sister. 'They wouldn't have kept him more than five minutes. Catching sight of him on the way in would have been more than enough.'

'Now, now,' said Mum. 'Think of your poor father.'

She was right there. One way and another it hadn't been Dad's weekend.

Anyway, he came out of hospital later that day, so all was well. In fact, he discharged himself. Apparently a team of doctors came to see him and he thought he heard one of them use the word '*amputer*'.

The man was looking at his leg at the time. Perhaps Miss Jones was right and they had their eye on him for spare parts.

'Not a day too soon,' said Dad when we met him in reception. 'I can't grumble about the food, but it's been costing me a small fortune.'

'You should have got an E111 card before we left,' I said. 'Max Masters says it entitles you to free healthcare under a reciprocal arrangement. I was reading about it last night.'

'Him again!' said Dad. 'There are some things I would rather not know.'

Anyway, I was glad we did go on an outing to Paris – otherwise I wouldn't have got the idea for my school essay. I bet the bit about Dad falling down the hole will have the whole class in fits, especially as we have a photograph of him being put in the ambulance. I might even get a star.

I bought my Big Sister a sticker of the

Eiffel Tower and she bought me a
bronze replica of it, which took
me by surprise. I think I
came off best. Why
anyone would want
to go around with
a sticker of the Eiffel
Tower on their chest I
don't know. I'd pictured it on
her bedroom wall. But she seemed very
pleased.

On the train going home we all agreed
that it was the best weekend ever.

Well, I say we all agreed. Dad was a
bit iffy because of the time he had spent
in hospital. There's another good thing
about it, though. Since we went to France
he has never once complained about my
not looking up when I am out with him.
It's quite the reverse now. He's the one

who keeps looking down. If he isn't careful he'll end up walking into a lamp-post, and I bet I know who will get the blame, so I'd better not say 'I told you so!'

In the meantime, Mortimer and I have a problem. I knew there was something wrong with him the moment we got back and I tried placing him in his drawer as usual. His little legs, which normally went nineteen to the dozen until he settled down, were as stiff as ramrods. The sun had been shining all the time we were in Paris and that may have had something to do with it. Perhaps he needs oiling, but if you ask me I think he needs winding up and I can't find the key.

My Big Sister may laugh, but she doesn't understand. It isn't her fault she was born with no imagination – I feel sorry for her. Even though he needs to be wound up regularly, Mortimer is flesh and blood to me, as real as real can be, and the best friend I've ever had.

Life wouldn't be the same without him. He's what you might call irreplaceable and he will just have to stay indoors until I find it. I'm sure he will forgive me – he's that sort of a pig – but I would never forgive myself if I had lost it for ever.

I'm sure Max Masters will come to my rescue. He's never let me down yet, and that sort of problem is just up his street. Like when he came across a tribe of abandoned robots in the Kalahari desert and got them all working again.

9

Trouble with the Oven

One day I had a really good chance to score what my dad calls Brownie Points, and would you believe it? I messed the whole thing up. It only goes to show that he's right about one thing. Just because something is on television doesn't mean to say it's true. It happened the night my Big Sister had her parents' evening and I was left to my own devices for a change.

My Big Sister's parents' evenings never last very long because none of the teachers can find much to say about her, except for things like Excellent and Well Done! Then, as ever, Miss Spooner says she is A Credit to the School. It makes you want to throw up.

Not like my parents' evenings, I can tell you. Mine go on for ever as the report is always left to the very end. Dad says it's because the teachers don't want to embarrass him and Mum in front of all the other parents. The teachers go on and on about my work.

Once I'd had to write an essay about a day in the life of a tortoise. Now, it isn't as easy as it might sound. I mean, if you're a tortoise, one day must be very like another. They never go to the cinema or read the newspapers or anything like that. If they kept a diary, they would have to put ditto marks on blank pages all the way through.

I wondered about writing a very short story about a tortoise that stayed in its shell all day because it was raining. Then I had what I thought was a GREAT IDEA.

Since tortoises probably can't write, except in a sort of spidery scrawl – or even spell very well for lack of practice, come to that – I thought that's how I should write it. It might get mistaken for the real thing – although it wasn't. As things turned out, I didn't even get any marks for neatness, which is what I usually rely on.

In fact, Miss Jones was quite worried. She thought I'd suddenly gone what she called dickslecsick, and for a time even the school doctor was concerned about me. I tried looking the word up in Dad's dictionary, but I don't think the man who wrote it knew what it was either. It was yet another example of trying to look up a word you can't spell. This time it took me four days! I think the man who wrote the first dictionary is to blame. Fancy knowing all those words and then not being able to list them properly.

You'll never guess how it's spelled . . . DYSLEXIC. Fancy having a word like that to describe people who have trouble reading! They would never find out what's wrong with them.

Anyway, I never go to parents' evenings – I only hear about them afterwards. They came home from the next one and Dad said: 'What's all this about our having to be rescued by helicopter from the top of the Eiffel Tower?'

We'd had to write an essay on our family holiday and it so happened that soon after we talked about going to Paris there was a James Bond film on television.

The other day I read that grown-up writers have something they call DRAMATIC LICENCE. That means they can change things around as much as they like. The trouble is, it's like getting a driving licence: no one under the age of seventeen is allowed one. If you use a dramatic licence before then, they say you are telling lies. That's something else which isn't fair.

I bet my dad would have been even more upset if I'd written a boring story about what he did last year instead of going on a proper holiday – he painted the front door! It took him a whole fortnight because people kept touching it to see if it was dry.

Mind you, schoolteachers are funny people. They can't know very much, otherwise they wouldn't keep asking you questions.

Anyway, after I'd listened to all the warnings about not opening the front door to strangers (last time I did I bought fifty dusters and the man told all his friends) and 'If you get hungry there are some cold sausages in the refrigerator, but make sure you leave some for the rest of us,' etc., etc., off they went to my sister's parents' evening.

It was as the front door was closing and I was opening the fridge door that I got this idea. I rushed upstairs to tell Mortimer. 'Why don't I have a nice surprise ready for them when they get back?' I said.

He seemed to think it was a good idea, so I rushed back downstairs again.

Well, I gave everyone a surprise all right, but it wasn't quite what they were expecting; nor me, for that matter. My idea was to have a meal ready for them. Mum's got this new cooker, you see, and I've been dying to have a go.

It's what's known as a 'State of the Art Catering Centre', whatever that means. It doesn't look much different to me, apart from the fact that it has TWO OVENS and a remote control module which sometimes switches on what sounds like a burglar alarm if you press the wrong button. I think Dad's right when he says he doesn't think it will ever fly. That made me laugh when I first heard it – the thought of an oven flying – but he says it to anyone who comes to the door now, including the man selling dusters. (At least it stopped him coming for a while.)

Anyway, just lately I've become very interested in cookery programmes. It seems to me that if you learn to cook you don't need to know about geography and history and mathematics and all those other boring things. All you need to do is open a restaurant and you can make lots of money. In fact – and here's another funny thing – you don't even need to cook. Some chefs are just rude to everyone – like asking them if they enjoyed their meal and then throwing them out if they say 'No'. They get famous that way. In fact, the more they do it, the more people go there to eat. I suppose they're hoping they may get thrown out too, then they won't have to pay.

I don't think I'd like to be that sort of chef, but I wouldn't mind having my own television programme. If you have your own television programme, you don't have to stay on afterwards and do the washing-up. I don't know whether you've ever noticed, but television chefs always have gleaming new pots and pans to work with. I've never yet seen a dirty one.

My mum had to get new ones after I'd finished cooking the meal, but that's another story. (Dad says she ought to be able to sue the makers under the Trade Descriptions Act for calling them 'non-stick'!)

I like Italian chefs best because they're always cheerful and make everything look easy peasy, which I suppose it is in a way: they have everything already chopped up for them before they start, so they don't waste any time. Though a lot of chefs chop things so quickly it's a wonder they don't cut their fingers off. I often wonder what would happen if they did – especially with colour television. If they chopped all their fingers off, I bet it would make the audience figures go up. But they wouldn't be able to do it twice, so it would be the end of the series.

Whenever Italian chefs cook something, they always start by pouring lots of olive oil into a pan, and then they throw all the ingredients into it. After that they empty a bottle of wine over the lot, give it a good stir and leave it to simmer while they go off to Italy to make a film. Or else, if they're short of time, they show the viewers round their herb garden.

Well, I could do that with my eyes shut.

Unfortunately I couldn't find any of the right ingredients to do something Italian, and I didn't fancy cold sausages cooked in olive oil, but I did find a tin of meat in the fridge, so I decided to make a stew instead.

It Wasn't Me

That was mistake numero uno (Italian for number one!).

Mistake number two was that because I didn't have as much time as I'd thought, instead of letting it simmer I turned the heat up to Mark 5. You wouldn't think water could disappear quite so quickly. I expect that's how George Stephenson got to be famous. He probably put some potatoes on to boil, then when the water dried up he thought: *Look at that! I've wasted all that steam. I bet I could have used it in an invention! I bet if I put some wheels on a kettle of boiling water it would pull people along. It might even go so fast I could call it the* Rocket.

Dad says some train companies are still using the *Rocket* to this day. Especially the one he uses to get to the office.

Anyway, I'd hardly finished peeling my

first potato when there was this funny
smell of burning from what used to be the
non-stick saucepan. Whoever designed it
had never tried making a stew. Mine got
so stuck to the bottom it wouldn't come
away, not even with one of Dad's wood
chisels.

Which was the very moment my
parents chose to arrive home!

'It doesn't matter,' I said, trying to
divert their attention by dropping a
dishcloth on Dad's toes. Then, doing
my best chef impression, I went to the
second oven, just like they do on television, and opened the door.

'Ta-daaa!' I cried. 'Here's one I made
earlier!'

And do you know what? There was
nothing there! So much for State of the
Art Cooking Centres – and so much for

television programmes! You don't know who to trust these days.

If you ask me, anyone who's a television chef needs to be a bit of a magician as well, but they never tell you that in their recipe books!

'It could have been worse,' said Mum when she discovered the open tin. 'We might have eaten it. You opened the cat's meat by mistake!'

Now, I don't know about you, but I'm not very keen on stories with unhappy endings, and there's nothing happy about an open tin of cat's meat – especially when you haven't had a cat for several years.

For me, the nicest ending of all would be finding something small that you thought you might have lost for ever.

Guess who found the key . . . My Big Sister! She's a funny girl. She didn't even tell me she was looking for it. Apparently it was buried in the carpet right by the chest of drawers. I must have been standing on it, and I know what she's going to say when I thank her: 'That's what comes of having such an untidy room.'

The thing is, I know she's right, but I can't help it. Besides, what matters most to me is poor old Mortimer. Imagine what he must have been going through: one moment lying on his back in the drawer with his feet in the air, unable to move; the next, still on his back, but with his little legs going nineteen to the dozen out of sheer joy.

I don't know about you, but I shall sleep better tonight!

Harry